First published in 2012 by
The Puppet Company Ltd
Units 2—4 Cam Centre
Wilbury Way
Hitchin
Herts
SG4 0TW

www.thepuppetcompany.com

ISBN: 978-1-908633-07-1

British Library Cataloguing-in-Publication Data
A catalogue record for this book is available
from the British Library

Printed in China

Three Billy Goats Gruff

Three Billy Goats Gruff

Re-told by Sue Lockey
Illustrated by Sandra Evans

Once upon a time there were three Billy Goats. One day they were grazing in a field eating some dry, tasteless grass.

Next to the field was a fast-flowing river, and on the other side of the river the grass was sweet and green.

"I am hungry and bored with this dry old grass," said Big Billy Goat Gruff.

"So am I," said Middle Billy Goat Gruff.

"So am I," said Little Billy Goat Gruff.

"Why don't we cross the rickety old bridge to the other side and eat there?" suggested Little Billy Goat Gruff.

They all knew that a huge, hairy, ugly Troll lived under the bridge and would eat them up if they crossed over his bridge.

Little Billy Goat Gruff was very hungry and longed to eat the sweet green grass on the other side of the bridge, so he decided to be brave.

Trip-trap, trip-trap, trip-trap, went Little Billy Goat's hooves as he trotted over the bridge.

Suddenly there was a loud roar and out jumped the Troll from under the bridge.

"Grrr, who is that trip-trapping over my bridge?" shouted the ugly Troll.

"It's only me, Little Billy Goat Gruff. Please may I go and eat the sweet green grass in the field over there?" But the angry Troll was not going to let him.

"I shall eat you up!" he roared. Little Billy Goat Gruff was very frightened, but he was also very clever.

"No, no, please don't eat me up," he said. "Middle Billy Goat Gruff is much bigger than I am, and he will make a much better and tastier meal for you."

The Troll agreed, and Little Billy Goat Gruff trotted over the bridge and began to munch the sweet green grass.

Soon Middle Billy Goat Gruff came along.

Trip-trap, trip-trap, went Middle Billy Goat's hooves as he trotted over the bridge.

Suddenly there was a loud roar and out jumped the Troll from under the bridge.

"Grrr, who is that trip-trapping over my bridge?" shouted the ugly Troll.

"It's only me, Middle Billy Goat Gruff. Please may I go and eat the sweet green grass in the field over there?" But the angry Troll was not going to let him.

"I shall eat you up!" he roared. Middle Billy Goat Gruff was very frightened, but he was also very clever.

"No, no, please don't eat me up," he said. "Big Billy Goat Gruff is much bigger than I am, and he will make a much better and tastier meal for you."

The Troll agreed, and Middle Billy Goat Gruff trotted over the bridge and began to munch the sweet green grass.

Soon Big Billy Goat Gruff came along.

TRIP-TRAP, TRIP-TRAP, went Big Billy Goat's large hooves as he trotted over the bridge.

Suddenly there was a loud roar and out jumped the angry Troll from under the bridge.

"Grrrrr, who is that trip-trapping over my bridge?" shouted the ugly Troll.

"It's me, Big Billy Goat Gruff. I have come to eat the sweet green grass with my two brothers, and I am not afraid of you!" said Big Billy Goat Gruff bravely.

With that, he lowered his horns, charged at the Troll and knocked him over the bridge and into the fast-flowing river.

He was never seen again!

Big Billy Goat Gruff continued to trot over the rickety old bridge and joined his brothers eating the sweet green grass.

Now they could go over the bridge whenever they wanted to, without having to worry about the Troll again and they all lived happily ever after.